I Like to Help My Mommy

By
Catherine Kenworthy

Illustrated by
Mary Alice Baer

A G... YORK
Western Publishing Comp... Wisconsin 53404

Text copyright © 1981 by Western Publishing Company, Inc. Illustrations copyright © 1981 by Mary Alice Baer. All rights reserved. Printed in the U.S.A. No part of this book may be reproduced or copied in any form without written permission from the publisher. GOLDEN®, GOLDEN & DESIGN®, A FIRST LITTLE GOLDEN BOOK®, FIRST LITTLE GOLDEN BOOK®, LITTLE GOLDEN BOOKS®, and A GOLDEN BOOK® are trademarks of Western Publishing Company, Inc. Library of Congress Catalog Card Number: 80-85083 ISBN 0-307-10107-X ISBN 0-307-68107-6 (lib. bdg.)
LMNOPQRST

Every morning Jamie and his mommy make a list of all the things they have to do.

"We're going to have a very busy day today," Jamie's mommy says.

Jamie doesn't mind. He likes to help his mommy.

He helps her make his bed.

Then he helps her
wash the dishes . . .

and sweep the floor.

When Jamie and his mommy finish a job,
they cross it off their list.
"What's next?" Jamie asks.
"Grocery store," his mommy says.

Jamie is glad. He likes to help his
mommy at the grocery store.

He helps her choose the best kind
of cereal.

Then he helps her at the check-out counter.

"Thank you," the cashier says. "Your mommy is lucky. She has you to help her."

"I like to help my mommy," Jamie says.

At home, Jamie helps his mommy put the groceries away. He knows that some things go in the cupboards . . .

and some things go in the refrigerator.

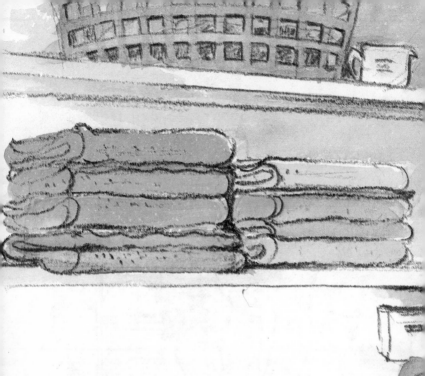

When all the groceries are put away,
Jamie helps his mommy do the laundry.
He helps her put the dirty clothes
in the washing machine.

Then he helps her hang the wet clothes
on the line to dry.

Jamie helps his mommy water the garden.

Sometimes Jamie's friend Bridget comes to play.

When they are finished playing, Jamie
and Bridget help by putting all the toys away.

Jamie likes to help his mommy make chocolate-chip cookies.

When the cookies are done, it's time
for one of Jamie's favorite jobs.

He helps his mommy eat them!